Henry Holt and Company, Inc.
Publishers since 1866
115 West 18th Street
New York, New York 10011

Henry Holt is a registered
trademark of Henry Holt and Company, Inc.

First published in the United States in 1996 by Henry Holt and Company, Inc.
Originally published in Sweden in 1996 by
Alfabeta Bokförlag AB under the title *Castor Syr*.
Library of Congress Catalog Card Number: 96-75137
ISBN 0-8050-4500-7
First American Edition—1996

Printed in China
1 3 5 7 9 10 8 6 4 2
The artist used watercolors and colored pencil
to create the illustrations for this book.

LARS KLINTING

BRUNO
the Tailor

HENRY HOLT AND COMPANY

NEW YORK

Bruno the beaver is a tailor.
His apron is very old and ragged.

Today Bruno will make a new apron for himself.

This is Bruno's sewing room. As usual, it is messy.
Bruno has trouble finding what he needs.

Aha! Here are the fabrics Bruno has been looking for.
Now he can get to work.

But this fabric is too thin.

And this fabric is too busy.

Bruno thinks this fabric is just right.

Before Bruno can begin sewing he must go to the laundry room.
He brings with him

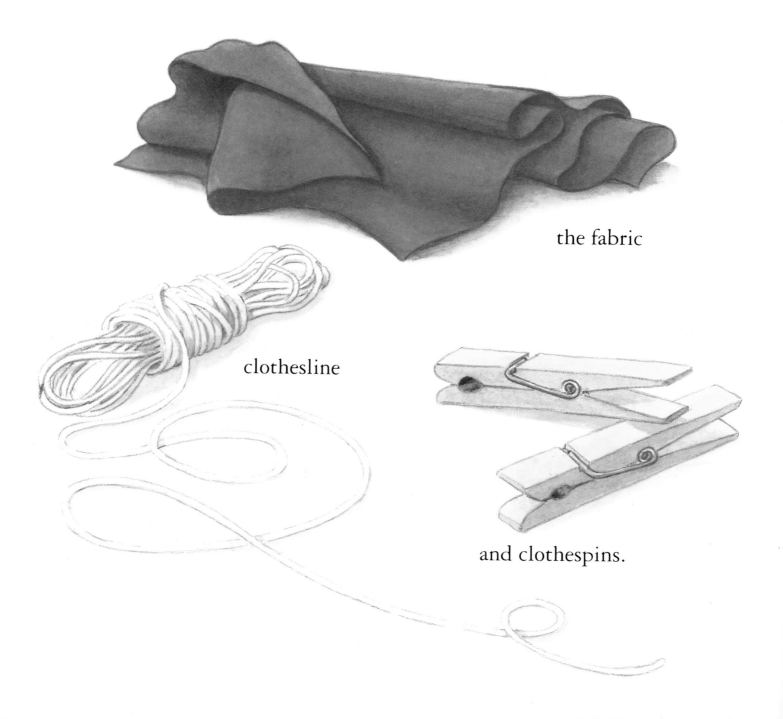

the fabric

clothesline

and clothespins.

First he washes the fabric in his washtub.

Then he hangs it up to dry.

While the fabric is drying, Bruno treats himself to a bath.

Next Bruno takes out

the ironing board

and iron.

He irons the fabric until it is smooth and flat.

Now Bruno will make a pattern. He gathers together

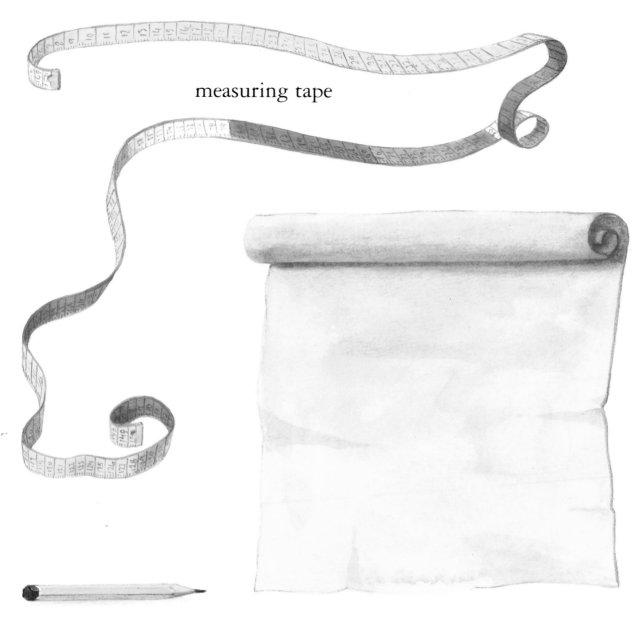

measuring tape

a pencil

and a piece of thick paper.

He takes his own measurements and draws a pattern on the paper.

Bruno will also need

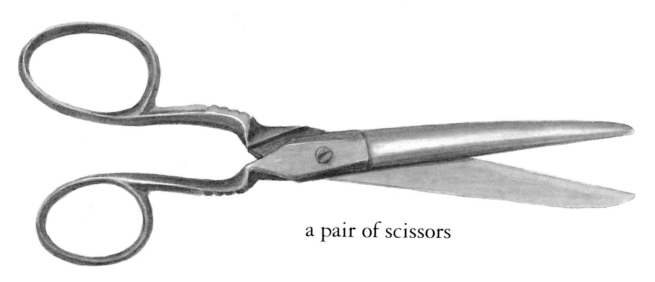

a pair of scissors

and a pincushion full of pins.

He cuts out the pattern

and pins it onto the fabric.

Then he cuts around the pattern.

Now he can start sewing.

It's time for Bruno to sew large stitches. This is called basting.
He will need

a spool of thread

a thimble

and a needle.

Bruno folds the edges of the apron and bastes them in place.
Then he bastes the pockets.

Ouch! Bruno pricks his finger on the needle.
After that, Bruno remembers to be careful.

The edges are basted and the pockets are where they should be.

The next step is to sew the pieces of the apron
together with straight, sturdy stitches.

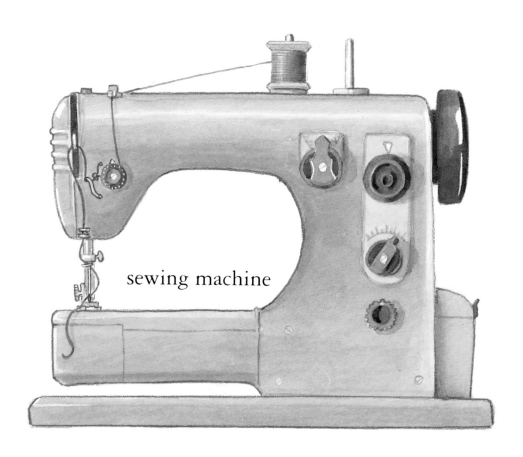

sewing machine

Bruno sits at his sewing machine.
He sews the edges. Then he sews the pockets.

Bruno needs to sew ribbons on the apron so he can tie it.
It takes him a little while to choose a color. Blue will do fine.

Bruno sews on the ribbons. The apron is almost done.
All he has to do is try it on.

Oh dear! It's too long.

Bruno cuts off a piece of fabric. Then he sews a hem
along the bottom of the apron with the sewing machine.

The apron is finished. Bruno the Tailor is
happy with his work. It's a perfect fit.

Bruno's Sewing Tips

PREWASHING

When fabric is washed for the first time, it often shrinks. Bruno washes the apron fabric before he starts sewing.

Before   After

BASTING

Bruno finds it boring to baste, but he knows it keeps everything in place when he stitches with the sewing machine. After Bruno finishes sewing, he removes the basting thread. This is easy to do, since he bastes with large stitches.

SEWING THE POCKETS

First he folds the upper edge of the pocket under twice and sews it on the sewing machine.

Next he folds the other edges under

and bastes each pocket onto the apron.

Then he sews over his basting stitches with the sewing machine. When he's done sewing, he removes the basting thread.

FINISHING THE EDGES

To be sure the edges of the fabric don't fray, Bruno turns the edges under twice and bastes them. Next he stitches over his basting stitches with the sewing machine.

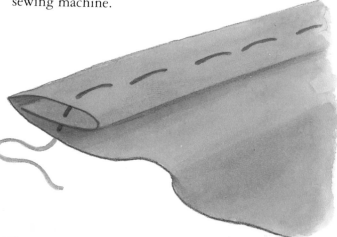

Bruno's Apron Pattern

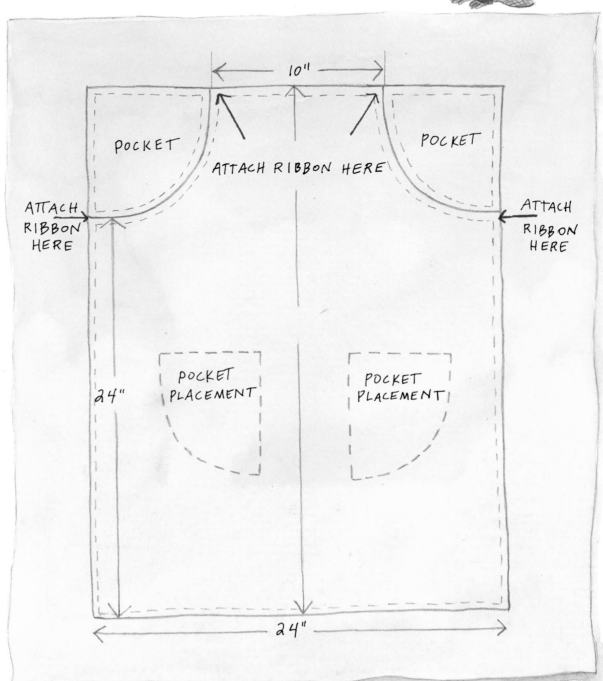

10"

POCKET

ATTACH RIBBON HERE

POCKET

ATTACH RIBBON HERE

ATTACH RIBBON HERE

24"

POCKET PLACEMENT

POCKET PLACEMENT

24"

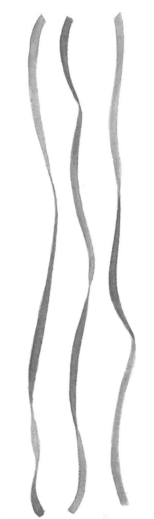

CUT THREE RIBBONS 20" IN LENGTH

Bruno's pattern won't be the right size for everyone, so be sure to take your own measurements before making your apron.